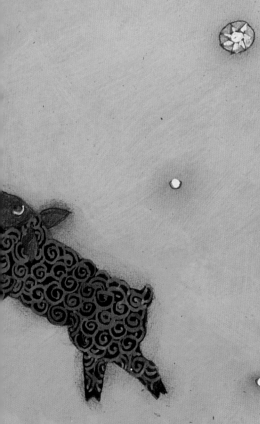

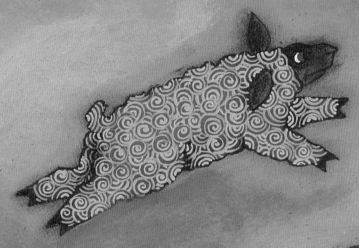

counting
ovejas

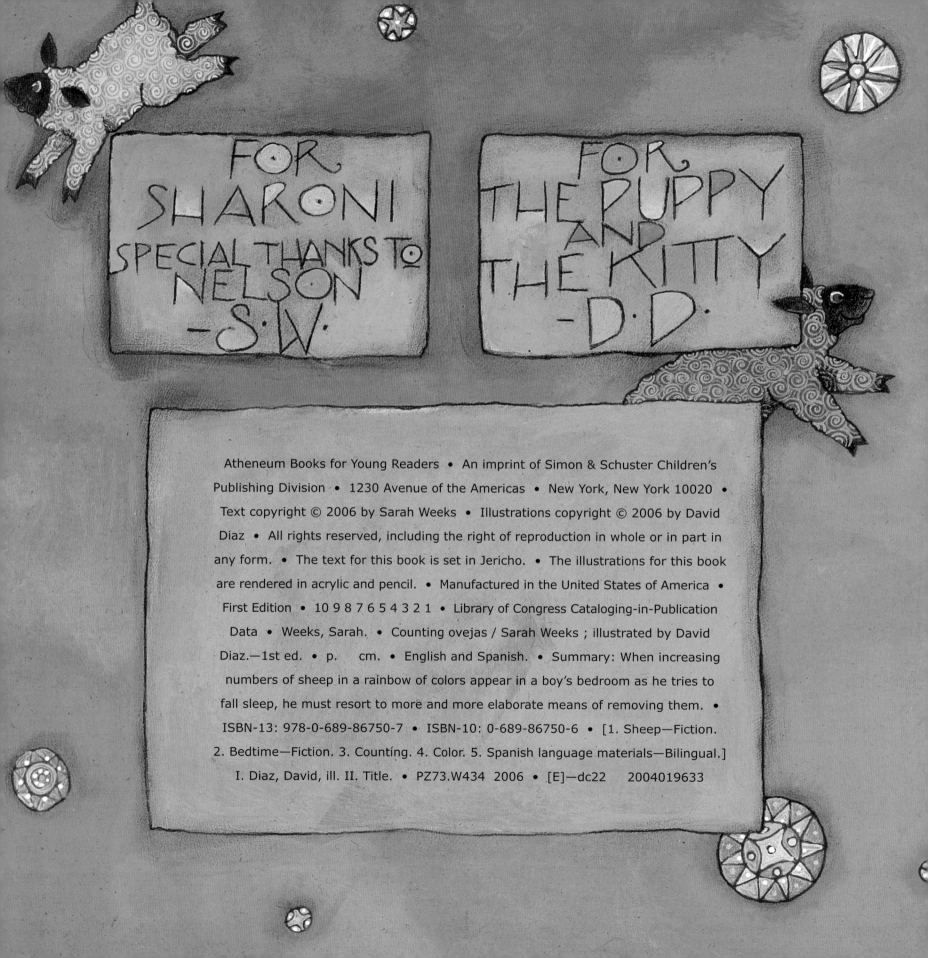

FOR SHARON!
SPECIAL THANKS TO
NELSON
—S.W.

FOR
THE PUPPY
AND
THE KITTY
—D.D.

Atheneum Books for Young Readers • An imprint of Simon & Schuster Children's Publishing Division • 1230 Avenue of the Americas • New York, New York 10020 • Text copyright © 2006 by Sarah Weeks • Illustrations copyright © 2006 by David Diaz • All rights reserved, including the right of reproduction in whole or in part in any form. • The text for this book is set in Jericho. • The illustrations for this book are rendered in acrylic and pencil. • Manufactured in the United States of America • First Edition • 10 9 8 7 6 5 4 3 2 1 • Library of Congress Cataloging-in-Publication Data • Weeks, Sarah. • Counting ovejas / Sarah Weeks ; illustrated by David Diaz.—1st ed. • p.   cm. • English and Spanish. • Summary: When increasing numbers of sheep in a rainbow of colors appear in a boy's bedroom as he tries to fall sleep, he must resort to more and more elaborate means of removing them. • ISBN-13: 978-0-689-86750-7 • ISBN-10: 0-689-86750-6 • [1. Sheep—Fiction. 2. Bedtime—Fiction. 3. Counting. 4. Color. 5. Spanish language materials—Bilingual.] I. Diaz, David, ill. II. Title. • PZ73.W434 2006 • [E]—dc22   2004019633

counting ovejas

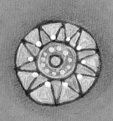
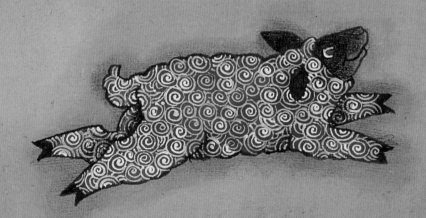

words by **sarah weeks**

art by **david diaz**

ATHENEUM BOOKS FOR YOUNG READERS

NEW YORK   LONDON   TORONTO   SYDNEY

Buenas noches. / Good night.
(bweh-nahs no-chehs)

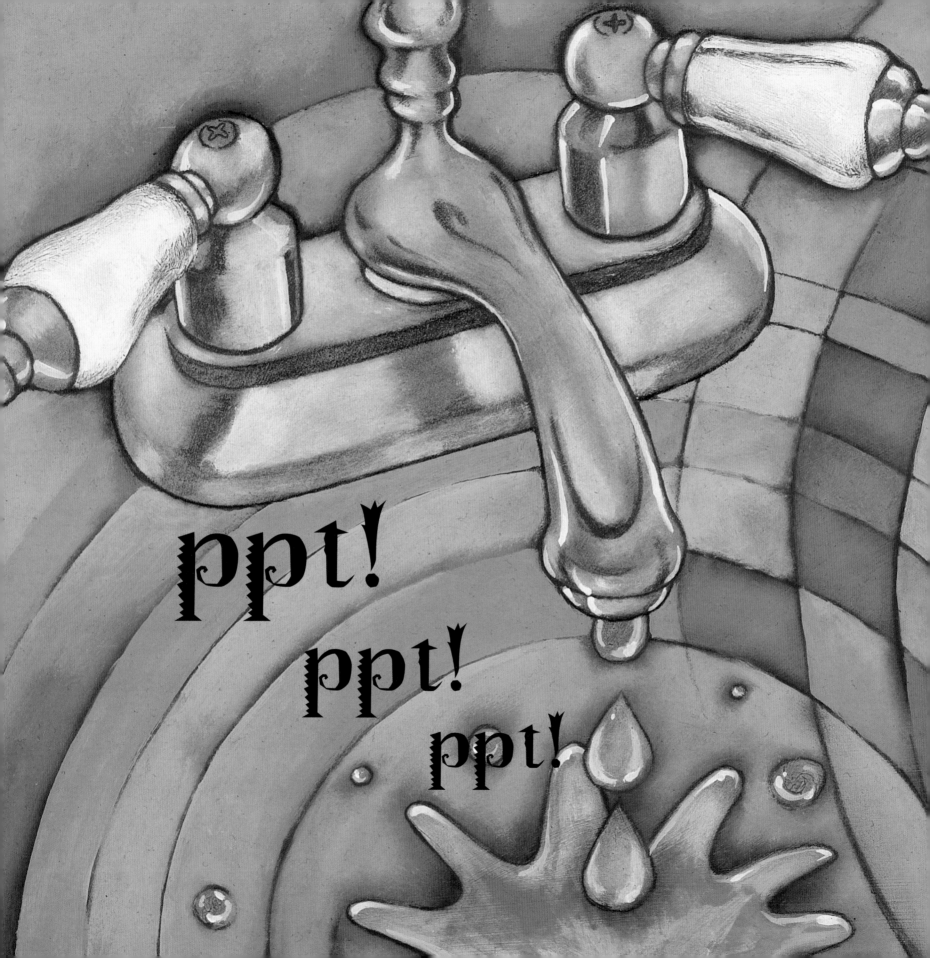

Una oveja blanca. / One white sheep.

(oo-na oh-veh-hah blahn-kah)

¡Adiós, oveja blanca! / Good-bye, white sheep!

(ah-dee-ohs, oh-veh-hah blahn-kah)

Dos ovejas marrones. / Two brown sheep.

(dohs oh-veh-hahs mah-rohn-ehs)

¡Adiós, ovejas marrones! / Good-bye, brown sheep!

(ah-dee-ohs, oh-veh-hahs mah-rohn-ehs)

Tres ovejas negras. / Three black sheep.

(trehs oh-veh-hahs neh-grahs)

¡Adiós, ovejas negras! /
Good-bye, black sheep!

(ah-dee-ohs, oh-veh-hahs neh-grahs)

Cuatro ovejas rosas. /
Four pink sheep.

(quah-tro oh-veh-hahs rroh-sahs)

¡Adiós, ovejas rosas! / Good-bye, pink sheep!

(ah-dee-ohs, oh-veh-hahs rroh-sahs)

Cinco ovejas verdes. / Five green sheep.

(seen-ko oh-veh-hahs vair-dehs)

¡Adiós, ovejas verdes! / Good-bye, green sheep!
(ah-dee-ohs, oh-veh-hahs vair-dehs)

Seis ovejas rojas. / Six red sheep.

(say-ees oh-veh-hahs ro-has)

¡Adiós, ovejas rojas! / Good-bye, red sheep!

(ah-dee-ohs, oh-veh-hahs ro-has)

Siete ovejas turquesas. / Seven turquoise sheep.
(see-eh-teh oh-veh-hahs tuhr-keh-sahs)

¡Adiós, ovejas turquesas! /
Good-bye, turquoise sheep!
(ah-dee-ohs, oh-veh-hahs tuhr-keh-sahs)

Ocho ovejas violetas. / Eight violet sheep.

(oh-cho oh-veh-hahs vee-oh-leh-tahs)

¡Adiós, ovejas violetas! / Good-bye, violet sheep!
(ah-dee-ohs, oh-veh-hahs vee-oh-leh-tahs)

Nueve ovejas azules. / Nine blue sheep.

(nweh-veh oh-veh-hahs ah-sool-ehs)

¡Adiós, ovejas azules! / Good-bye, blue sheep!

(ah-dee-ohs, oh-veh-hahs ah-sool-ehs)

Diez ovejas amarillas. / Ten yellow sheep.
(dee-ehs oh-veh-hahs ah-ma-ree-yahs)

¡Adiós, ovejas amarillas! / Good-bye, yellow sheep!

(ah-dee-ohs, oh-veh-hahs ah-ma-ree-yahs)

Gracias, ovejas. / Thank you, sheep.

(gra-se-ahs, oh-veh-hahs)

Buenas noches. / Good night.

(bweh-nahs noh-chehs)

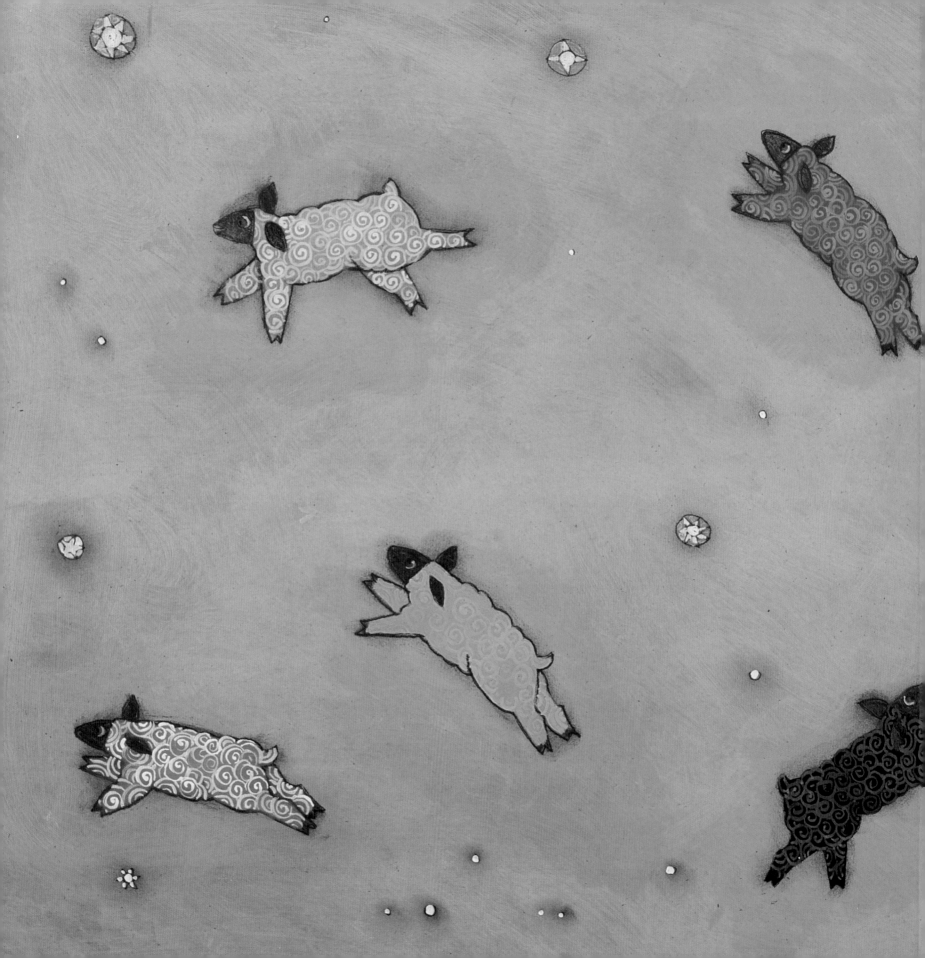